THAT'S WHAT THE NOTHING HEADS SAID

That's What the Nothing Heads Said

TERRY LANCASTER

A finger pointing at the moon
A message in a bottle
A smoke signal you left behind
So that one day you might follow

Wabi sabi, Kemosabe

In the land between the rivers

In the time before the flood

The Nothing Heads lived in paradise

Growing taters in the mud

No mud no taters

That's what the Nothing Heads say

Squishing mud between their toes

All the livelong day

There were hardly any left those days

The Nothing Heads were down to a few

That didn't bother them awfully much

There wasn't awfully much to do

Happy Hollow was a pleasant place

The Nothing Heads pleasant and kind

Living in little hillside huts

Built from whatever they could find

The flowers grew bright and pretty

The grass grew green and tall

The Nothing Heads danced and sang loudly

Being still inside most of all

But in the land of Woodashoodakooda

In the time that never was

The Woodashoodakoodans were never happy

With the way that anything does

They were angry about one thing or another

Complained about this and that

But mostly about the others

They hated them from way back

If the others would only listen

If they'd only do what we said

We wouldn't be in this predicament

With this sword above our head

We could be living lives of luxury

Living high up in the hills

Eating caviar from gallon jars

Wiping our butts with dollar bills

Now we have to work and work

To have anything hardly nice at all

It's because those stinking others

I can't stand their stinking gall

Meanwhile deep in the capital confines

They were cooking up a plan

Led by Bossy Big Boss McBosserson

The Grand Poobah of all the land

And Secretary of Commerce McRicherson

Richy knew all the tricks

For turning squiggly lines into dollar signs

For turning chestnut trees into toothpicks

The two of them had commissioned a report

They'd formed a progress committee

They'd honed their pitch and pleaded their case

In every town and every city

We're sick of those stinking others screams
Bossy

Tired of carrying their load

It's time we teach them a thing or two

About paying what bills is owed

We have to protect our rights yells Richy

The water's on our side of the line

The others are taking advantage

Trying to take what's mine

We're gonna stop the river they announced

We're gonna build a dam so high

It'll hold almost enough water

To last a thousand lives

Our people will never grow thirsty

Our fields will never go dry

Our crops will grow taller than chestnut trees

That reach into the sky

The dam will turn the engines

That make the sparky sparks

And light up Woodashoodakooda

So we never face the dark

With all those sparks we'll build factories

So everyone has good jobs

We'll make doohickeys and doodads

Thingamajigs AND thingamabobs

We'll party hard one day a week

On the world's most enormous lake

If we work like mad six others

All you can do is all it takes

Work hard play hard

That's what folks say

In the land of Woodashoodakooda

As they work their lives away

If those others put their back into it

If they put their nose to stone

They could have stuff too

Nice stuff of their own

But they don't so they shouldn't

And why do they even care

If they're not gonna use it

Why shouldn't we put a lake there

All those tall trees just standing

Think of the things we could make

We can build our dam and factories

Cut down the forest to build a lake

If the others don't like it

Well that's just too stinking bad

Thems that had their chances

Shoulda took the chance they had

So the people of Woodashoodakooda

Gave it all they could

They cut down each and every tree

Sawed it up real good

They used all the pieces and parts

Everything but the squeals

Every little splinter fueled another

Of Richy's rickety deals

They made the dam from tall tall parts

Toothpicks from the branches

Which Richy sold in most every flavor

In most markets and most circumstances

Waste not want not Bossy printed

On paper made of leaves to boot

Well that makes sense they all said

They even dug up all the roots

They burned the roots for sparky sparks

The dam never made enough

For all the factories that they needed

To make all their shiny new stuff

And all across Woodashoodakooda

They built bigger and bigger houses

With room for all their treasures

All their grumbles all their grouses

Room for all their toothpicks

Locked in climate-controlled crystal racks

Can't risk the others

Getting their grimey paws on our stacks

Everyone had their own and private

Tricycle built for two

Riding alongside each other

Shouting about what they should do

If they only had just a few more toothpicks

They could head to the lake and play

That sure would be awesome

Maybe some other day

Hi ho hi ho off to work they go

And the stuff they had was great

But the six days of work they'd been promised

Had somehow turned into eight

Since everyone was working so hard

With no time at all for play

Richy McRicherson sold them helpful robots

For just a few dollars a day

For a few dollars more

The robots would tell you the time

So you'd never be late for work

So you could turn every minute into a dime

The really nice robots

Well their price was quite dear

They could wake you up in the morning

And whisper gently in your ear

Have you tasted the latest toothpicks?

You deserve the best

You work hard so you don't have

To settle like all the rest

Then out the door the robots shooed them

With a reminder to work extra hard

The McJonesersons just got a new garden 'bot

To beautify their yard

The robots entertained them

Told them all the latest news

Like what Bossy Big Boss was doing

To make the others pay their dues

The robots told them stories

About the way things used to be

And how things were going to get better

Just you wait and see

About all the stuff the factories were making

How Richy was building a paradise

With homes so big you'd never

Go in the same room twice

About the new tricycles for next year

With luxury seating for four

Or just the one and lots of shiny stuff

From Richy's Shiny Stuff Superstore

Coming soon were robot trikes

That the robots drove for you

So you can do more of the kinda stuff

That Woodashoodakoodans liked to do

Which wasn't much of anything

The Woodashoodakoodans just hurried back and forth

From home to work and to the store

Going all in for all they were worth

The sooner we can get there

The sooner we can skidaddle

The Woodashoodakoodans said

As they loaded up for battle

Every day was a competition

To see who came in first

To judge the days by numbers

Who was best who was worst

Who tasted the fanciest toothpicks

Who drove the fastest trikes

And whose houses had the strongest locks

To keep them safe at night

The robots told them the score each night

As they drifted off to sleep

Today was nowhere near good enough

Tomorrow you'll have to dig deep

The dam was soon 10,000 feet high

The lake 10,000 miles long

All the forests and all the trees

Were soon used up and gone

All the factories in Richy's chain

Needed sparks to keep them going

With all the trees gone missing

Ain't no more roots growing

All the water in the lake

Was supposed to turn the gears

But Richy had been conserving water

And hadn't done that in years

The gates had rusted shut

The water couldn't flow

And was now spilling over top

With nowhere else to go

With no more logs to build it higher

With no more tar to mend its leaks

The dam probably wouldn't last much longer

Than a mere handful of weeks

Richy and Bossy sounded the alarm

They raised a great hue and cry

Those dirty stinking others didn't do their part

They didn't even try

Charts and graphs showed the danger

Richy and Bossy showed the map

All the robots had a countdown function

With a tickety tic toc app

We've only got a matter of weeks

Until the dam's gonna blow

Until the lake says catch you later

You no good so and so

For 10,000 miles upriver

Nothing but smokestacks blowing naught

We have to go downriver screamed Bossy

It's the only chance we've got

We'll be reasonable with the others said Richy

Reasonable to a limit

But we have to save that dam

It's our water itn't it?

An exploratory committee was formed

A scouting party assembled

Diplomats and bankers

And the well-dressed sales clerks they resem-
bled

Richy sent along toothpicks

From the premium VIP collection

Only the finest flavors

From Richy's personal selection

Lawyers most of all

Was definitely what was needed

To explain how all the forests downstream

Would soon have to be untreed-ed

They brought along the tree-ologist

The one that they could find

To explain how all of this was best

For all of treedom's kind

But just in case they brought soldiers

In case the others wouldn't listen to reason

In case they needed to make

A different kind of appeasement

One by one they assembled

At the dam's tippity top

One by one they ambled

Down the 10,000-stair drop

Days and days it took

For the whole team to arrive

Then a few days more accounting

The necessaries to survive

The Woodashoodakoodans had never been downstream

They'd never even thought to look

They'd all read about the great forests though

In all the great history books

Richy and Bossy sent a robot along

For data and communication

To keep them fully updated

And apprised of the situation

We've got to be ready for anything said Bossy

Or so the robot read Bossy's lines

Bossy was behind locked doors

Safely in the capital confines

At the bottom of the dam

Where the river used to flow

The Woodashoodakoodans headed downstream

Robots clocking them as they go

At 10,000 steps per hour they stated

At 10,000 steps per mile

We'll be deep in the forests in no time

Each step closer brings a smile

They all kept their heart rates up

Thumpety thumpety thump

With robots giving reminders

When their pacing needed a bump

We need to go further faster yelled Richy

At least Robot Richy did

The real Richy McRicherson

Was well and safely hid

In the world's largest bathtub

By the world's largest lake

10,000 miles upstream shouting

We have to give it all it takes

Step by step downstream they went

At least where the stream used to be

There wasn't much of a river down there

At least not that they could see

A little mud at the base of the dam

But that quickly disappeared

And the further downstream they wandered

Things became worse than they'd feared

There was no river left to speak of

No river meant no shore

No fish no bank no forests

No tall trees no more

As far as the eye could see

All they could see was clay

Baked as hard and dry as bones

Basking in the sun all day

It was forests they were seeking

Trees to feed the beast

But there weren't any trees here either

Which meant trouble at the very least

Bossy had a conniption

A hissy and a fit

It's those dirty stinking others

They're the cause of this

They didn't do what they oughta

They didn't do their share

If they loved those doggone trees so much

Why have their forests gone bare?

All the robots in Woodashoodakooda

All the tickety tocking screens

All the proclamations from the capital

All said the very same thing

On one hand was the dam

Crumbling and giving way

10,000 miles of water

Just waiting for the day

On the other hand wastelands

10,000 miles of dust

And the army of Woodashoodakooda's

Exploratory bust

Richy had a conference call

With all the robot wranglers

The wheelers and the dealers

The bright and shiny star spanglers

The Woodashoodakoodans have no work to do

They've barely anything to eat

They're buying so few toothpicks

Our sales goals we'll never meet

Not that we have any toothpicks to sell

We still can't find any trees

And when the dam blows it's over

Said the Deputy Assistant Deputy VPs

What about my water? cried Richy

How many tubs can I fill?

Who's eating or not ain't my problem

They've still got to work the till

They're no better than the others

Always making up excuses

We should build robots to replace them all

Replace all their useful uses

That's it Bossy exclaimed

Go get the Chief Tiddlywinker

We'll get the robots to find the trees

Thanks to our brightest thinkety thinker

Dr. Smarty McSmartypants then explained

About the robot in the sky

The one flying above Woodashoodakooda

With the super zoom zoomity eye

We've been watching Woodashoodakooda

For all the Woodashoodakoodans' good

Tracking tricycles and toothpicks

Tracking every scrap of wood

We know who's been good or bad

We know who's wide awake

We know who's been working hard enough

For Richy & Bossy's take

We know everything there is to know

About everything there can be

In the land of Woodashoodakooda

We believe in what we can see

But we don't know nothing about nothing

About whatever's happening over there

About the great forests and the others

We hadn't the attention to spare

But if I tinker and I twiddle said Smarty

If I do so just right

If I twist the dials and turn the knobs

Throughout all of the day and most of the night

I think that by morning

I can have the robot flying downstream

Maybe have the camera zooming farther

Than eyes have ever seen

There's only one problem

One tiny little hitch

To see deep into the forest

Everyone's channel has to switch

Every screen in Woodashoodakooda

Every signal every sign

Has to be tuned in and showing

Whatever it is that we find

So they figured and they fiddled

All through the night

They dialed in all the frequencies

And by dawn's early light

Every robot in Woodashoodakooda repeated

Your attention is required

Almost everybody looked to see

What might then transpire

But they still couldn't see far enough

To see where they needed to see

Someone isn't paying attention cried Smarty

That's the only thing it could be

Smarty's contraption was powered by attention

The closer you looked the more you'd find

But if everyone was looking at everything

It just scrambled up the mind

We have to check the data flow

We have to calibrate the transponder

We have to see who's watching what

So we can see over yonder

But with the spy cam pointing outward

They had no way to understand

Who was or wasn't paying close attention

To the urgent matter at hand

Sporty McSporterson was anxiously checking

Updated statistics and real-time scores

Newsy McNewserson couldn't stop talking

About economic markets and wars

Nothing to see over there

Busy McBizzerson said

Ain't nobody got time for that

I gotta do this instead

Preppy McPrepperson was making plans

In a hurry and just in case

What if they don't find any trees

We've got to get out of this place

The laggards and the stragglers though

All eventually tuned in

The eye in the sky grew stronger

Looking farther than anyone had ever been

We kept our part of the bargain

We lived the Woodashoodakoodan dream

Why didn't they just do what we did

Or come up with their own kinda scheme

They just up and quit playing

Took their whole ball of wax home

What are we supposed to do now

Now that we're in this all alone

I guess that's it said Bossy

Our goose is good and cooked

If we didn't want to see what we saw

We shouldn't have lookety looked

I give said Richy

My water's as good as gone

The river's going to run again

I've nothing left to count on

All across Woodashoodakooda

Everyone just let go

For everything they had built and seen

They had nothing left to show

No one was coming to save them

Nothing was going to last

It was all over but the shouting

And the shouting was coming fast

Except it didn't

There was hardly any fuss at all

So it's like that? they asked

All that rises must fall

Gone gone gone far beyond

Beyond where anyone could tell

Way way off in the distance

No One dinging a bell

Woodashoodakooda stopped breathing

Silent in stunned disbelief

Then the bell dingety ding dinged again

And they all sighed in relief

But the buzzers went buzzing crazy

The clackers went clackety clack

Every robot in Woodashoodakooda screamed

Woodashoodakooda is under attack

The others are making their move

Look out here they come

They've always wanted what we have

Now they're taking some

But there was nothing on the screen to see

Nothing but sky and clay

The bell kept on dinging though

All the livelong day

There's nothing there to see said Smarty

But there's definitely something there

You can almost just kinda make it out

If you look a little less more just kinda stare

So they all stared

Each and every one

They let their minds go blank

Until nothing was left undone

Until there was nothing inside their heads at
all

No river no dirt no sky

Until they couldn't even remember

What they were even trying to find

For just a moment they quit thinking

Quit looking for something to find

For a split second they just were

Like they'd powered down their mind

Then someone saw it

What they'd never seen before

Standing right there out in the open

Like it had been there forever more

It's a bird it's a plane

I finally see the light

I can't believe it's been here all along

Hiding out in plain sight

It's a sign from above said Preachy McPreacherson

Our destiny and birthright

Looks dangerous to me said Sneezy McSneezerson

How does this aid our plight?

It's definitely more water said Richy

That's definitely what I see

Choppy McChopperson asks

Is that like a tree?

A single tree a stack of stone

A few squiggly lines

Maybe some kind of door or something

Maybe some kind of sign

Maybe some kind of map

By an old forgotten path

Maybe an old description

Of a new kind of math

None of which explained

Why that bell was dinging

Or why they all could now

Apparently hear singing

Asiagi

Kemosabi

Jijimuguy

Bodi soho

Asiagi

Kemosabi

Jijimuguy

Bodi soho

Nothing stirred in barren starkness

As Woodashoodakooda stood guard

Then bam out of nowhere

Something hit the camera hard

Two giant red eyes

And crooked beak filled every screen

Wake up screeched the hawk

Then peck nothing is all that was seen

Darkness fell on Woodashoodakooda

Every robot screen went blank

Every whirling whirly gig

Went clankety clank ker plank

Every robot whirred to a stoppety stop

Every light suddenly went out

The sun went down with no moon to be found

Woodashoodakooda's silence was louder than
a shout

They couldn't see what they'd all seen

But they all still heard what they heard

Aciagi Kemosabi

They just understood not a word

Then hello said No One

Welcome to Happy Hollow

We're glad you found the bread crumbs

Left out for you to follow

We knew you would eventually

Everyone always does

Everyone becomes No One

Same as it ever was

Who do you think you are yelled Bossy

I demand to know

I'm the Big Boss of Bosses

I'm the one running this show

That's cute said the voice

How you think someone's in charge

And that that someone is you

That's a leap quite large

Who are we? No One

No One not even a little

Same as you just passing through

Playing both ends against the middle

We don't know nothing about nothing

We have nothing that you seek

Nothing here to worry about

Nothing here to see

Nothing but figments of your imagination

Just a thought that you thunk up

A thought that says more about you

Than it ever could about us

Poppycock yelled Bossy

You're one of them dirty stinking others

You've been planning this all along

And now you've got your druthers

There are no others Kemosabi

There is no us and them

We're all in this together

Each each other's whim

We're pretending to be this

You're pretending to be that

With all this pretending going on

We forget where it's really at

If we weren't playing pretend

We wouldn't be separate kinds at all

It's all fun and games of course

Just chewing gum and having a ball

We're all the same kind of kind though

That's the kind we are

Kind of like the same kind of jelly

In a different kind of jar

What the actual fudge are you even talking about said Richy

Just point us to the nearest trees

We need toothpicks and tar and caviar

And roots and bark and leaves

Trees aren't really something

That you can pick and pull apart

When you're pretending to be a tree

That makes for a difficult start

Trees are for sleeping under

And waking up under too

Trees turn sunshine into shade

That's what trees do

But pretending to be a tree

Takes a very very long time

You have to commit yourself to it

You have to make up your mind

There's just the one tree now

The one we're waking under

If you stick around long enough that is

Without going all asunder

I'm not trying to be a tree you idiot

Are you some sort of clown?

If Woodashoodakooda's going to be safe

We have to cut them down

We need to sell more toothpicks and stuff

We need logs to block the flow

When we have all the stuff we need

Maybe then we'll let some trees grow

Woodashoodakooda could never be safe

There's no such thing as enough

There's no way you could ever

Not need more stuff

That's the nature of stuff

There's other stuff that it's not

There's the kind of stuff you have

And the kind you haven't got

The trick about stuff is seeing

It's all just more of the same

The only noticeable difference

Is once you give it a name

Everything is everything said No One

Nothing is as it seems

Only words make it look separate

Helping us get lost in the dream

The wordy words are good

for understanding and explaining

But they trick us into thinking

It's the truth that we're naming

The map is not the territory

The menu is not the meal

The finger and the moon it points at

Are not at all the same deal

Words are castles built on sand

Their meaning is always changing

Between the writer and the reader

And the dance that they're arranging

Sand castles of course

They always tumble down

Here we are left living

In a world without any nouns

The facts of the matter are this said Smarty

E equals mc squared

Math is math numbers don't lie

It's how we stay prepared

The math ain't mathing said No One

The only thing math can do

Is describe the very same thing

That we invented it to

But ask any scientist

Ask the ones with prizes

Make them swear to tell the truth

Ask them what the big lie is

Reality isn't real

Is what they'll have to tell ya

There's no there there

Stuff is just what they're trying to sell ya

Matter doesn't matter

There is no matter to mind

Right now is all that matters

And the peace that we may find

If you're not there to look at something

There's nothing there to see

What there is to look at

Depends on what you be

Relativity-ly speaking

It's all just opinions we made up

Nothing there at all

Worth getting your panties in a bunch

One way or another

That's the way things are all along

Saying one way is right

Just makes the other way wrong

On again off again

A dash then a blip

A digital snake eating

The tail of its own tip

The chase is what makes the game

So fun to play along

It's easy to forget we're singing though

And get lost in the song

Blasphemy yells Preachy McPreacherson

You're gonna get in trouble

Talking that talk in a construction zone

Your fines are gonna be double

Construction and destruction said No One

Are just the ins and outs

Without one there is no other

Of this there is no doubt

Chasing the good and fleeing the evil

Merely keeps you in chains

Freedom is the realization

That you're the whole stinkin' game

Home is where your feets is

If you can keep your head there too

There's nowhere else to go

There's nothing left to do

This is the Happy Hollow

The lull between the waves

The momentary lapse between future and past

The eternal now the end of days

The space between this and that

The land without pride or shame

Where everything is everything

And nothing has a name

So is you is or is you ain't?

Time to choose which one to be

A whole lot of something you thunk up

Or a whole lot of nothing to see

It's impossible to say of course

Which one of these is real

The this that you can speak of

Or the that that you can feel

It's you who decides

In which place you want to live

Only you can choose

Which two hoots to give

You can dwell forever in Happy Hollow

If you can empty out your head

Rejoice in the way things are

Without longing for something else instead

That's nonsense says Splainy McSplainerson

Make believe magic and voodoo

I ain't buying that at all

You've got some 'splaining to do

There's nothing to explain there Splainy

You couldn't if you tried

It's too far gone beyond anything

Wordy words can describe

Abawa Cadabawa

With these words we doth create

But once we bite the apple

We're deep deep deep in the game

It's nothing but magic after that

A subtle sleight of hand

Pretending things are the way ain't

Just singing along with the band

The old razzle dazzle

A shimmy and a shake

Watch what one hand is giving

Don't look at what the other hand takes

It's a trick we're playing on ourselves

A game of hide and seek

Trying our best to prove others it

So we don't have to be

Looking for ourselves in a big stack of others

Looking for something that proves

That we're the something special

That we've got something to lose

But we're nothing special

We're no thing at all in fact

We are all of this and nothing more

The motion not the act

All of this said No One

Gesturing broadly in the dark

Thou art this

Infinite eternal spark

Peace then whispered No One

Twice and once again

The whispiest whispered whisper

There's ever ever been

The lights flickered back on

The robots gently whirred

And Woodashoodakooda pretended to forget

Whatever it was that just occurred

Richy and Bossy kept on

About finding trees for the dam

Dr. Smarty McSmartypants kept twisting dials

For audio and cam

The robots reminded Woodashoodakooda

About the dangers they all faced

It's time to get back to work

Building and protecting this place

Hippy McTripperson and the Flower Children

Started planning a groovy trip

Diving deep down the rabbit hole

Looking for clues and tips

High up on Pumpkin Ridge

Grouchy and Sneezy were at it once again

Arguing about this and that

Same as it's ever been

Fluffy McFlufferson's tail though stopped fleeing

And Fluffy stopped giving chase

And a tiny sly smile and sparkle

Snuck up on Fluffy's face

Staring at the robot screen

Fluffy could now see clear as day

What that was down by the river

What it was it had to say

Seek not the Kingdom

Said the sign big and bold

Seek not the Treasure

From tales long foretold

Seek not the answers

To questions large and small

Those who enter Happy Hollow

Shall seek no thing at all

Fluffy yawned and stretched

Rolled over once or twice

It wasn't much of nothing

But it sure felt nice

The End

Written by Terry Lancaster

Here Come

the Nothing Heads

An epic poem for children of all ages, **Here Come The Nothing Heads** tells the tale of Sneezy McSneezerson, Grouchy McGroucherson, and Fluffy McFlufferson who live in the fanciest pumpkin high atop Pumpkin Ridge, but they are banished by town Elders because they can't get along with each other or anyone else.

They must travel to Happy Hollow, home of the mysterious tribe of Nothing Heads, and learn how to live in peace. The trials and tribulations of their adventure force them to look at life in a brand new way that was as old as time itself.

BeKindClub.org

*Nadalada Was
a Nothing Head*

Hippy McTripperson travels the world looking for answers to life's big questions in this whimsical prequel to **Here Come the Nothing Heads**. Lost in the desert, then lost at sea, Hippy eventually loses it all in a strange land down by the river.

That's when the Nothing Heads begin to arrive in Happy Hollow, each seeking something completely different and each finding the one thing for which they never even thought to look.

BeKindClub.org

The **Be Kind Club** publishes books, audiobooks, and videos - available on our website and at some of the coolest bookstores, gift shops, and roadside fortune-teller stands ever (Amazon & Audible too).

When you join the club, you get free access to all of our titles in digital and audio formats, free Be Kind Club apparel, and wholesale pricing on printed books.

We're big fans of seeing the big wide world do as the big wide world likes to do. Here are a handful of our favorite places to sit and watch.

- *Friends of Land Between the Lakes*
- *Friends of Cross Creek National Wildlife Refuge*
- *Friends of Warner Parks*
- *Friends of Harpeth River State Park*
- *Friends of Shelby Park & Bottoms*
- *Big South Fork National River & Recreation Area*
- *Dr. Julian G. Bruce St. George Island State Park*

Your membership helps us support them. Thanks.

BeKindClub.org

www.ingramcontent.com/pod-product-compliance
Lightning Source LLC
Chambersburg PA
CBHW030634120726
47904CB00006B/2152